A CAPTAIN NO BEARD AD

BEING A CAPTAIN
IS HARD WORK

Written by Carole P. Roman
Illustrated by Bonnie Lemaire

For Hallie, you are the calm in stormy seas, a voice of reason in chaos.

Captain No Beard stood on the deck of the Flying Dragon and watched his crew hard at work.

Mongo was up in the mainmast; Hallie was swabbing the deck, and Polly was bringing pretzels to the crew while Cayla was stuffing holes with rags, and young Zachary was preparing to raise the flag. It had the promise of a great day, Captain No Beard thought proudly.

"How does it look?" the captain called out to Mongo, who was peering through his telescope.

"I think we have some rough seas ahead, Captain. I see some dark clouds, and the wind is whipping up something fierce."

Captain No Beard scanned the horizon. A storm wouldn't match well with his plans. He needed to get to Dew Rite Volcano by dark. It was straight ahead. He pulled out his spyglass and looked at the sky.

"I don't see storm clouds, Mongo. Those are cumulus clouds. They don't mean anything," he commented, dismissing the white clouds in the sky. "They are fluffy and white, like great balls of cotton. Everybody knows those clouds don't bring rain."

Mongo glanced back at the sky; his face concerned. "I, um, I don't know, Captain. I think they are pretty dark and dense. I think they are *strato*cumulus, and they mean rain."

Captain No Beard shook his head. "I don't believe so, Mongo. I know my clouds, and these don't mean rain. I think we're good to go. Come down from the mast and prepare to set sail."

Mongo looked at the choppy seas and groaned.
"It's getting pretty rough out there. Are you sure, Captain?"

Captain No Beard didn't reply; he turned to get Polly's attention.

"Fire up the galley, Polly. I'm in the mood for some chocolate pudding!" the captain ordered.

"Fire up the galley!" Fribbet repeated from his spot on a barrel.

"Are you sure that's wise, Captain? The ship is rocking pretty badly!" Fribbet jumped so high he hit his head. "Ouch!" he shouted.

"Avast, Fribbet!" the captain ordered. "I think you are overreacting. Don't let me suggest a time-out," he warned.

Hallie stopped her swabbing to watch the darkening horizon. Her lips trembled. She didn't like the way the sky looked.

"You know, Captain. Mongo may be right; those clouds do look stormy," she said

"I'm the captain, and I think I know what's best for my ship." Captain No Beard paced the deck, his arms folded across his chest.

He looked at Linus, who held the wheel.

"Full speed ahead! Dew Rite Volcano is due north," the captain bellowed.

Linus looked at the large shape of the volcano, then at the captain's set face. "I think it's more westerly than north."

The captain gave him a stern look.

"Aye, aye, Captain," the lion agreed unhappily.

Captain No Beard approached the the youngest crew mate.

"Let's raise the colors, Zach!" he ordered.

Zach looked at the sky then back to the captain.

"Don't you think the wind is too strong?"

Captain No Beard shook his head.

"I think I know the wind better than you, Zach."

"I don't know; the sea looks pretty rough," Zach said.

The captain pointed to the flag and then the mast.

Zachary saluted and hoisted the flag up the pole.

The ship caught a gust of wind and lifted high above the sea.
They surged ahead. Cayla lost her footing, flying upwards.
Only Matie's quick reaction by catching her by one of her
horns saved the little girl.

The sea swelled, raising the ship so that it hung suspended in midair, landing with a bone-jarring crash.

Polly flew up from the galley, a smoking rag clutched in her claw. "No can do, Captain. The pudding tipped; I almost had a fire, and now the galley is a mess. There is burned pudding everywhere. It looks like Dew Rite Volcano erupted in the galley!" the parrot said in a breathless rush.

A leak sprouted from the ship's side.

Cayla ran to plug it with an old burp cloth.

She stamped her foot on the hole with a grumpy expression.

"We are going too fast; a storm is coming, and it's getting cold!"

Cayla yelled.

"Don't be a baby. It's a little salty water," the captain laughed.

Everyone stopped working and stared at the captain,
their faces filled with concern.

"Stop your worrying. I'm the captain. I know what I'm doing,"
he explained confidently.

They moved forward, the ship lurching, picking up speed. The wind burned their cheeks, making their eyes water from the sting of it.

The lump of Dew Rite Volcano loomed like a dark triangle ahead of them. Hallie looked behind her. The sky had closed up so that she couldn't see where they had been.

Hallie shook with fear.

It was getting icy. Cold droplets misted around them, making the deck slippery. Cayla's legs flew out from underneath her. Fribbet, Cayla, Mongo, and Matie started to glide along the shiny deck.

"Swab faster," the captain ordered when he saw his sailors sliding along the ice-covered deck.

Hallie struggled with her mop. It was frozen to the wood.

Polly glanced up at the flagpole, pointed, and let out a loud yelp.
"Zach!" she cried.

Everybody turned to see Zach holding onto the mast with one hand, the torn flag clutched in his frozen fingers.

"All hands on deck!" the captain shouted. "What are you doing?"

Zach looked down, his eyes wide with fright. "It was being ripped away by the wind. You told me I always had to protect our flag," he called out over the rising seas. "My hands are getting numb!" he cried. "I can't hold on much longer!"

"Shiver me timbers!" Hallie screamed, running to the bottom of the pole.

There was no time to think; he had gotten them into this mess, and he had to get them out of it.

Captain No Beard yelled, "Hold on, Zacky! I'm coming to get you!"

He jumped onto the pole, climbing faster than any other time in his life. The wind snatched his hat. The wood was slippery from the spray of the towering waves.

Hallie watched, her breath stuck in her throat.

The ship swayed dangerously from the rough seas.

The crew cheered when he reached the top.
The captain grabbed the little crew member, and together
they inched down the mast to safety.

The flag lay on the floor. It was torn and limp.

The crew looked at the crumbled heap, then to Dew Rite Volcano, and finally at the captain. They were not happy.

Captain No Beard glanced at their sad faces. He gulped and opened his mouth, "Being a captain…"

"Don't even think about saying that," Hallie interrupted.

"Well, it is hard work," the captain stated. "I have to make all the decisions. I have to choose what's best for us."

Hallie looked at him with a hard stare.
"Why do you think you have two ears and one mouth, Captain?"

"Hmmm," he responded.

"Two ears?" Mongo repeated.

"One mouth?" Fribbet hopped around. "What about the nose?"

"Two ears so you listen twice as much as speaking!" Hallie told him.

Captain No Beard thought about it.
His first mate was making a lot of sense.

"Listen, Captain. You have surrounded yourself with many experienced hands. We are here to help you," Hallie explained.

"But I'm the captain. I know everything!"

Cayla shook her head. "You didn't know about the clouds."

Fribbet jumped up and down. "You didn't know the direction to Dew Rite Volcano."

Zach touched the flag with his bare foot. "You didn't know the weather was too rough for raising the flag."

"And you wanted that chocolate pudding and didn't consider the consequences of rough seas and fire!" Polly squawked.

The sea started to calm, but Captain No Beard's face was troubled. He was the captain. He was supposed to know everything. He started this voyage confident that he did.

"I think I did wrong in my quest to go to Dew Rite Volcano," the captain said sadly. "I was pig-headed and stubborn as a billy goat."

Matie made a loud noise, clearly insulted.

"Sorry, Matie. I was stubborn like a little boy who thinks he knows everything."

"You didn't do anything terrible, if you learned something, Captain." Hallie put her hand on his shoulder.

Captain No Beard looked at his crew, his shipmates, the people he had chosen to join him on his adventures.

"Nobody knows everything," Hallie told him with a smile. "A good friend will always tell you when you are doing something wrong."

"It's up to me to listen twice as much then," the Captain said.

The crew all nodded in agreement. "Arrrgh, arrrgh, arrrgh!"

The sea stilled as it turned back into carpet; the ship rocked to a stop, and the clouds evaporated to become bedroom walls once more.

"Whew! That was some adventure," Cayla sighed.

"You can say that again," Alexander responded.

" Whew, that was some adventure," Hallie repeated with a giggle.

"I may be captain, but I learned a wise leader listens with both ears, so he can learn as much as he can and make the best decisions for his crew."

" Our crew is lucky to have such a smart captain," Hallie told him.

"Aye, me hearties! I have the best crew that ever sailed the seven seas!" Captain No Beard agreed.

Cloud Key

- Altocumulus (Al-toe-cu-mu-lus) - heavy gray and blue cover of clouds consisting of water and ice at middle altitudes.

- Altostratus (Al-toe-stra-tus) - Middle altitude clouds that often look like a flat, gray sheet over the sky. The sun or moon can sometimes be seen shining through, but may appear unclear.

- Cirrocumulus (Cir-roe-cu-mu-lus) - A cloud that forms at high altitudes and can look like ripples in the sky, usually meaning fair but cold weather.

- Cirrostratus (Cir-roe-stra-tus) - High altitude clouds made up of ice crystals. The sun or the moon can shine through the clouds, sometimes with a halo-like effect around it.

- Cirrus (Cir-rus) - Ice clouds that are tall and light. Usually found in clear skies, Cirrus clouds can mean nice weather. Don't be fooled by these clouds, as they can sometimes mean the weather's changing, too.

- Cumulonimbus (Cu-mu-lo-nim-bus) - Huge clouds soaring to great altitudes, leading to thunderstorm conditions. Heavy rainfall, gusts of wind, hail and lightning are sure to come when seeing Cumulonimbus clouds.

- Cumulus (Cu-mu-lus) - Puffy clouds that look like cotton candy and regularly develop throughout sunny days.

- Nimbostratus (Nim-bo-stra-tus) - What's in a name? In Latin "nimbus" mean rain and "stratus" means spread out. Nimbostratus clouds form at low altitudes with light rain over a widespread area.

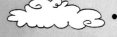

- Stratocumulus (Stra-toe-cu-mu-lus) - Gloomy, thick clouds filled with tiny water drops at a low to lower-middle altitude. Stratocumulus clouds come with a chance of snow or rain.

- Stratus (Stra-tus) - Low layer of clouds that are stretched out across the sky. Stratus clouds show an overcast sky and can come with a chance of light rain, sprinkle or a light, short shower of snow.

28348532R10035

Made in the USA
Middletown, DE
12 January 2016

Hawaii

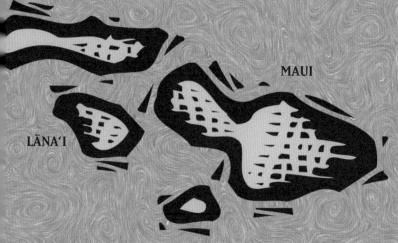

MOLOKAʻI

MAUI

LĀNAʻI

KAHOʻOLAWE

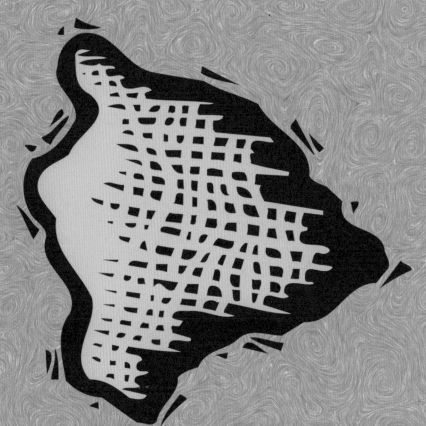

HAWAIʻI

KIMO'S SURFING LESSON

Written by Kerry Germain
Illustrated by Nicolette Moore

Book design: Carol Colbath

ISBN 0-9705889-2-5

ISBN 13 978-0-9705889-2-7

Island Paradise Publishing All rights reserved.

P.O. Box 163

Hale'iwa, Hawai'i 96712

www.surfsupforkimo.com

Printed in Korea

First Edition—First Printing

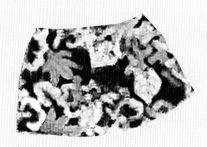

This story is dedicated to my niece Paulina.

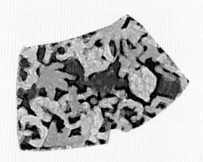

"I can't wait to surf!" Kimo said. "The waves are perfect and everyone's going." He tossed his backpack on the table where his mother sat pulling a plumeria blossom down a long string.

"**W**ho are you making that lei for? Oh no, I forgot, cousin Katie comes today!"

"We're picking her up at the airport in an hour," Kimo's mom said.

"I finished all my homework at school so I could surf!" he said. "Pleeeese!"

"Sorry, put on a clean T-shirt and get ready to go."

Kimo plopped down on his bed where his cat Scrapper lay curled up.
"I don't even know her. I'll bet she's a girly girl," he said.

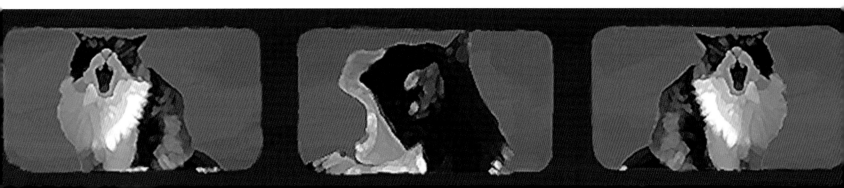

"**B**ummer, no surfing *and* I have to play with a girly girl."
Scrapper just yawned. Why did Katie have to come today?

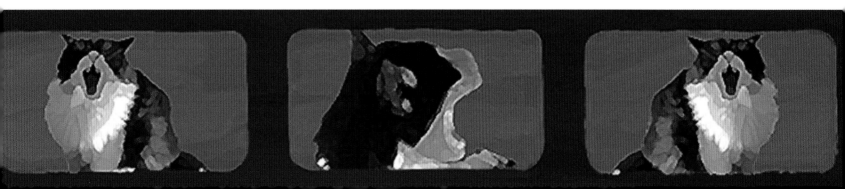

"Let's show Katie some Aloha Spirit while she's here."

"How long will that be?" Kimo asked.

"Only a few days. Then she's off to Maui to visit Auntie Mona."

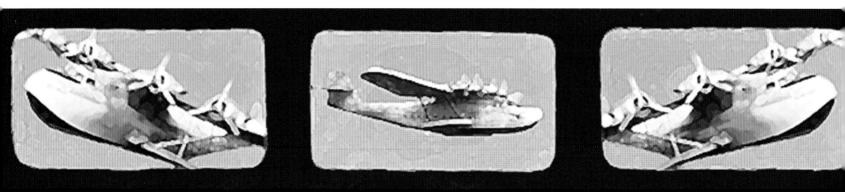

"**K**atie!" shouted Kimo's mom. "What a big girl you are flying to Hawai'i all by yourself." Kimo placed the lei around her neck. "Aloha."

"Aloha," Katie said politely as she smelled the flowers.

Katie was wearing a dress with matching ribbons in her hair. Even her shoes and socks matched.

"**W**hy don't you two go surfing when we get home," Kimo's mom said.
"I want to but I don't think she will." Kimo mumbled. Katie's smile turned upside down. It was a long ride home.

"Aloha Katie," said Kimo's brother, Kawika.

"What's up cousin?" said Kimo's other brother Pono. "Do you play basketball?"

"A little," replied Katie.

Kimo raised a brow. Pono passed her the ball.

Katie took a deep breath. She raised her hands up, held the ball like a real pro, and threw it. Kawika tried to jump out of the way but the ball hit him in the back, nowhere near the basket. Kimo could hardly contain himself. Girly girl, he thought.

Katie gasped as she covered her mouth. Her face turned bright pink.

"I'm sorry," she said. "It's hard to shoot in these clothes."

"Sure it is," said Kimo, smirking.

Katie picked up her bag, stomped past him, and marched into the house.

A few minutes later Katie came outside dressed in shorts and a T-shirt. She hopped right into the game, stole the ball from Kimo, and took a shot.

"Three points!" she yelled.

"She's on my team," Pono said.

Katie glared at Kimo.

"Still think I'm a whimp?" she said. "It was the dress, wasn't it? Just because
I like wearing a dress doesn't mean I can't play sports."

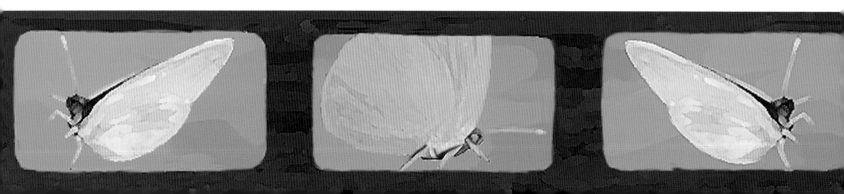

Kimo passed the ball to Katie.

"Then, do you want to go surfing?" he asked.

Katie let out a big holler.

"*Woo Hoo!* I thought you'd never ask."

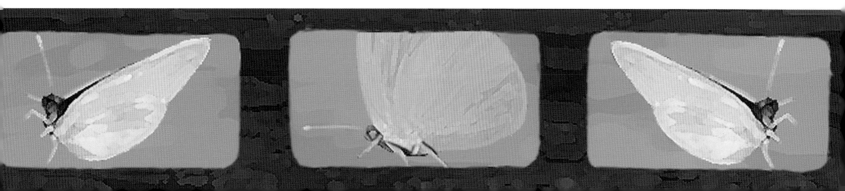

Kimo threw Katie a pair of board shorts. Then he ran to his room, put on his trunks, and grabbed some surf wax. When he saw Katie, he tried not to laugh.

"Do I have to wear these ridiculous things?" Katie asked.

"They'll keep you from losing your bathing suit or getting a rash."

Katie sighed. "Okay."

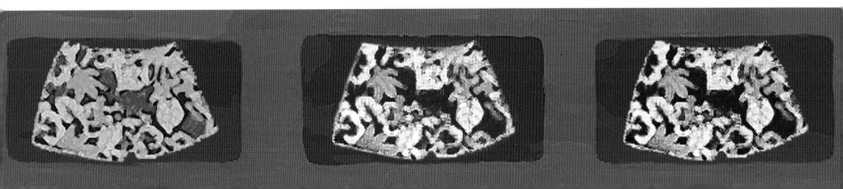

Kimo took Katie to the side of the house to find her a surfboard. A rainbow of colored boards stood side by side.

"This one's perfect for you," Kimo said.

"What?" said Katie. "You picked the ugliest old board on the rack."

"It might look bad, but I bet you'll stand up on it."

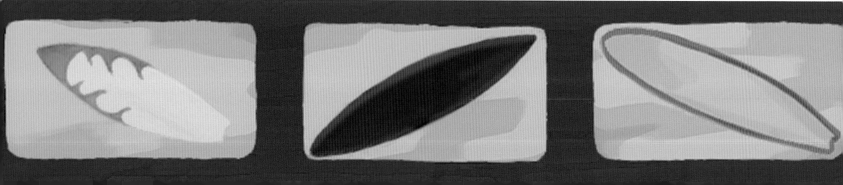

"**I** don't know," she said. "Maybe this is not such a great idea."

"Okay, why don't you go put that dress back on and come watch me surf."

"No way! Give me that board."

At the beach Kimo waved to his friends. Katie tried to keep up and struggled with her board.

"Let's sit here first and watch what the waves are doing," Kimo said.

Katie watched a kid ride a wave all the way to shore. When the surfer got closer, she noticed it was a girl.

"Wow! She's good," Katie said.

"That's Keala and yeah, she's real good," he said.

"**K**eala, this is my cousin Katie, she's visiting and wants to try surfing."

"Hi," Keala said. "You can swim, right?

"I'm on swim team at home," Katie said. "But that's in a pool."

"We'll start with the inside whitewater." Kimo said.

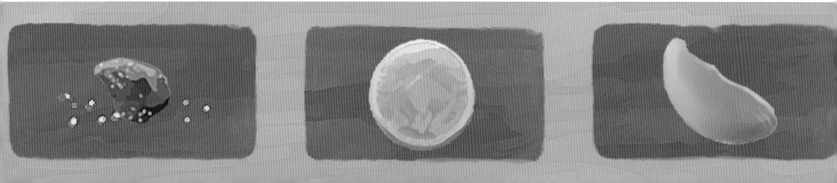

Kimo waxed up his board then planted it straight up the dry sand. When Katie's board was waxed and ready, they waded out into the water. Keala paddled out ahead of them.

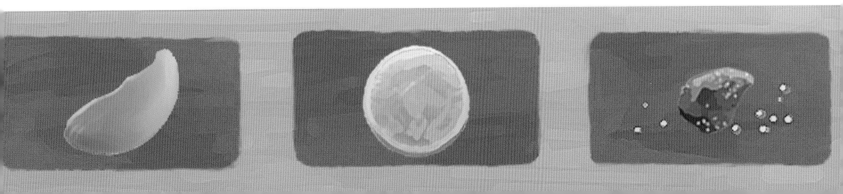

Kimo turned the old long board around to face the beach.

A wave of white water was fast approaching.

"Hop on and I'll push you in," Kimo said.

"Hold on. Ride it on your belly, okay?" said Keala.

"Okay!" yelled Katie.

W*hoosh!* Katie clung to the board. She felt like she was flying. Suddenly the board flipped. Katie crashed into the foaming water while the board kept surfing without her.

On her next attempt she waded out into knee-deep water, flattened herself on the board and tried to paddle. Her arms stroked the water, but she barely moved. Kimo bodysurfed in to meet her. He showed her how to paddle.

"Get ready!" Kimo hollered. "Head straight for the beach. Look for my board," he said pushing her into another wave.

Whoosh! Katie sped along. She felt the wax grip her body and tried to stand. Instead she was pitched into the soup. Saltwater rushed straight up her nose.

By the time Katie made it back out she saw Keala surfing across a wave.

"Wow, I wish I could do that," she said.

"Keep trying and you might," Kimo said.

Katie tried wave after wave. Wipe out after wipe out until she was drained. Slowly she paddled for the beach.

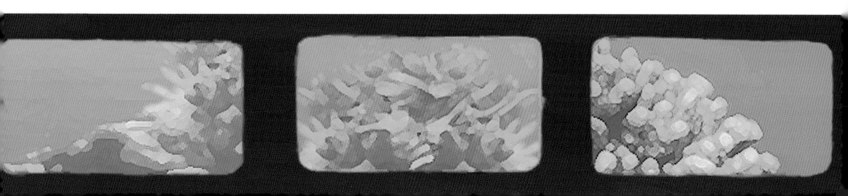

"Giving up so soon?" Kimo asked. "I guess girly girls quit faster."

"What! I'm no quitter!"

Katie turned her board around and paddled back out, digging deeply
with each stroke.

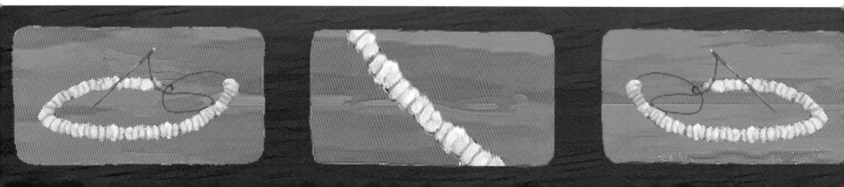

"Here comes one," called Keala paddling by. "It's got your name on it!"
Katie slid her board into position. She was ready for the whitewater to take her.

This time she didn't hesitate. The moment her board raced out in front of the water, she stood up. Balancing with her arms, she rode standing all the way. "Yes!" Kimo shouted.

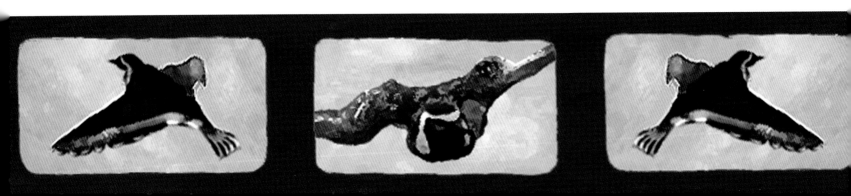

Katie rode wave after wave. Once she got the hang of it she didn't want to stop. The last of the day's sun shimmered on the water when the van drove up.

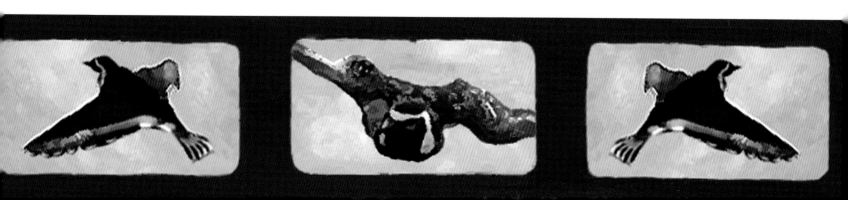

***B**EEP BEEP!*

"One more!" Katie begged. "One more!"

"Lucky for us it's Aloha Friday," Kimo said. "We can come back tomorrow."

"Promise?" Katie asked.

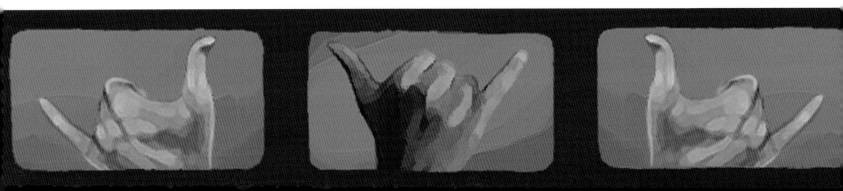

"**P**romise," he said. "Maybe we can pick up a new pair of board shorts."

"Thanks," Katie said. "But these work fine, as long as we come back."

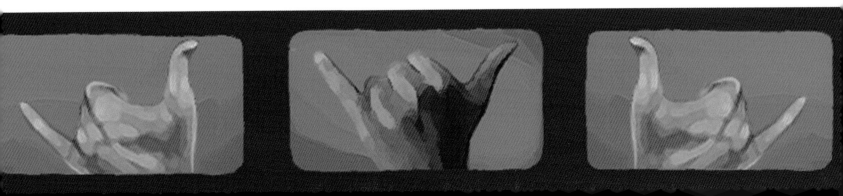

"I think we can do both," Kimo said. "We'll catch some good waves in the morning."

"**Y**es! Katie said. "I can't wait to surf again!"
Kimo picked up one end of Katie's heavy board.
Together they walked to the van.

PRONUNCIATION GUIDE

Here is a little something to help you with the Hawaiian words. The Hawaiian language is gentle and smooth to the ear. Whether you live here, on the mainland, or abroad, here are some guidelines to help you with this beautiful language.

VOWELS
- ❀ A sounds like (ah) as in above.
- ❀ E sounds like (eh) as in wet.
- ❀ I sounds like (ee) as in tree.
- ❀ U sounds like (oo) as in dude.

K and P about the same as English but with less aspiration.
LMNO about the same as English

W Hawai'i (hah wai ee) or (ha vai ee) when w follows an a it sounds like w or v. Both are acceptable.

w Hale'iwa (ha lay eva) w after i sounds like v. Kawika (Ka vee ka)
w Kuwili (koo wee lee) w after u and o usually sounds like w.

The 'okina (glottal stop) is a consonant. It signifies a breath break, "oh-oh, I broke it."

Stress or accent in Hawaiian pronunciation is usually placed on the next to last syllable. An exception to the rule occurs when a kahako (macron) is shown above a vowel (mālolo), which is then treated with the greatest stress.

In 1978 is was declared that English and Hawaiian shall be the offical languages of Hawai'i.

BORDER FUN FACTS

Plumeria
This fragrant blossom has been name "Kimo" by North Shore author and plumeria expert Jim little. Plumeria trees are found in many Hawaiian yards but are not native to the islands. The trees or shrubs come from the West Indies and are now found across tropical America. The word Plumeria was named after the French botanist Charles Plumier (1646-1701). To find out more read *Growing Plumeria in Hawai'i* - by Jim Little.

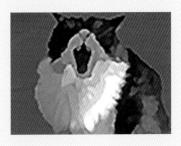

Tuxedo Cat
Scrapper is a long hair tuxedo cat. Have you seen him in our other books? *Surf's Up For Kimo* and *Kimo's Summer Vacation*.

   To be considered a tuxedo cat, its black coloring should be solid throughout, with white limited to the paws, belly, chest, throat, and chin. The tuxedo cat should appear as if the cat is wearing a formal tuxedo suit.

Honolulu International Airport
The first civilian flight from the mainland took place in 1927 from Oakland, California. They crash-landed on Moloka'i, but made it. In 1936 Pan American Airlines flew passengers from San Francisco to Hawai'i aboard the flying boat—a Martin 130. Commercial Jet service came in 1960 with service between the mainland and Hawai'i.

Hibiscus Flower
This bright yellow flower, *Ma'o hau hele*, is native to the Wai'anae mountains on O'ahu. It is also the State flower for Hawai'i.

Hawai'i Basketball
Honolulu-born Luther Halsey Gulick Jr. contributed to the invention of the basketball in 1891. Gulick was born in 1865. Hawai'i's first basketball games were held at the Honolulu YMCA in the late 1890's. The first outer island game was played on Maui in 1907. In 1990, Jennifer Kaeo became the first woman basketball player from Hawai'i to join the Olympic Festival's women's basketball team.

Rooster— *Moa Kane*

History suggests that the first settlers arrived around 500A.D. from the Marquesas Islands bringing with them the first chickens. Five hundred years later the Tahitians arrived bringing a larger and much more colorful rooster. Unlike other colorful birds, ownership was not limited to *Ali'i*—royalty. However, rooster feathers were used on top of the *kahili* torch which usually signified royalty was present.

Butterfly

This new species, the Large Orange Sulfur, was first reported on Maui in the spring of 2004. It was probably introduced accidentally as larva on plants shipped from the Southwest. It is common in Arizona and is now abundant on all the islands. It varies in size. Most are about the size of a quarter.

Board Shorts

Board shorts or trunks for boys and men have been around since the 1950's. Styles and fabrics have changed over the years. The girls line of board shorts came about in the 1990's with a comfortable fit made for girls and women. At one time some surfer girls wore the boys shorts to protect them from getting a rash or losing the bottom part of their bikini. Today they are a fashion statement in and out of the water. They can be seen on surfers and non-surfers around the world.

Surfboards

Boards made from foam blanks have been around since the 1950's. In 2005, epoxy resin boards or boards with hollow cores gained popularity due to Clark Foam, the biggest maker of foam blanks, going out of business. Many surfers refer to that day as Black Monday.

Lifeguard Tower

A beacon of safety. Lifeguard service on O'ahu began with two men on Waikīkī beaches. Today, O'ahu Ocean Safety and Lifeguard Division consists of 193 men and 7 women. The women are required to take the same physical test as the men. To find out more on these living heroes's read: *Rescue in Paradise* by David W. Doyle

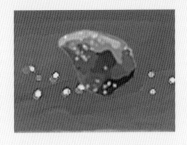

Surf Wax

Wax is essential for surfing. Without it you'd slide right off your board. Surfers used Parowax, made from paraffin in the 1950's because home-makers kept a supply on hand to seal jams and jellies with. Today, there are over 150 kinds of wax to choose from. This small bar of wax has a colorful past. To find out more read: *Surfboard Wax— A History* by Jefferson Wagner.

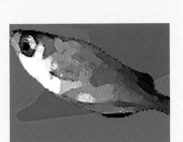

Aholehole Fish

The Hawaiian *aholehole* (*Kuhlia sandvicensis*) is restricted to coastal waters throughout the Hawaiian Islands. Its maximum length is about 30 cm (12 inches). Favorite ways to eat this fish are dried, or broiled on hot coals, also salted or *ho'o melumelu*. It can often be seen in schools jumping out of the water escaping from predators.

Bodysurfing

Bodysurfing is the art and sport of riding a wave without the assistance of any buoyant device such as a surfboard or body board. Bodysurfers tend to have a modest attitude toward wave riding and consider their sport to be more pure than other forms of riding waves. Some surfers in Hawai'i have stated that they use bodysurfing as conditioning for big wave riding.

Coral Reef

The first traces of coral reefs date back more than 500 million years. Coral reefs serve as a habitat for fish and other sea animals. They too are living and are also responsible in part for how the waves break in Kimo's back yard. To learn more check out: www.surfing-waves.com

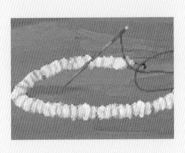

Puka Shell

This shell comes from the disc end of a cone shell that has been tossed and tumbled in the surf and sand over time until all that remains is the cupped top. The Hawaiian word for hole is *puka*. The *puka* in the center of the shell is naturally worn through making it perfect for stringing a necklace. Surfers from Hawai'i have been wearing these necklaces since the 1960's.

Plover— *Kōlea*

These small birds fly non-stop 2,700 miles across the open ocean to Alaska to breed. In August, they fly back to Hawaii. They make the trip in two days and travel at speeds up to sixty miles an hour. Fossil clues tell us this migration flight has taken place for at least 120,000 years. To find out more read: *Kōlea* by Marion Coste.

Shaka

The "shaka" sign means everything from "right on" and "thank you" to "howzit" and "hang loose". A local lore is that it originated with Hamana Kalili of Laie, who lost the middle three fingers on his right hand during an accident at the old Kahuku Sugar Mill. Because he could no longer work in the mill, he became a security guard on the sugar train that traveled between Sunset Beach and Ka'a'awa. One of his jobs was to keep all the kids from jumping on the train to ride from town to town. The kids started signaling each other the "all clear sign" by making the shaka. Since the security guard Kalili lost his fingers, it was the perfect signal to notify all that he was not in sight.

VW Van

The ultimate surfmobile since the day the VW van rolled off the assembly line and debuted in the Geneva Motor Show in November 1949. By the early 1950's, the van made its way to coastlines around the world. Surfers are free to travel with their boards from surf break to surf break while taking along a place to sleep and eat. The promise of perfect waves and another sunny day awaits the surfer cruising down the highway in the VW van.

Mahalo Nui Loa

Author Kerry Germain

As this book revealed itself and took on a life of its own, it happened to be full of female power, from cousin Katie to the women involved in its creation. Mahalo to: Claudia Cannon for sparking the idea. My fantastic writers group, The Sisterhood of the Traveling Pens, Ronda Taylor, Jennifer Crites, and Fumi Carpenter. Illustrator Nicolette Moore and book designer Carol Colbath. Thank you all for your insight, blunt critique and teamwork. Not only did you share your talents with me but your ability to laugh and enjoy our time together. Being with you never felt like work, I will always be grateful and will look back with the fondest of memories.

I'd also like to thank Jim Denny author of *Hawai'i's Butterflies and Moths* for the unpublished information on the orange sulfur butterfly.

Of course none of the above could have been possible without my biggest supporters— my husband Mike and son Jack who inspire my creativity and give me space, now and again, to let it ride.

Illustrator Nicolette Moore

I have to thank God first and foremost for all the blessings he's bestowed upon me, including this one. Thanks, Kerry for this wonderful opportunity. I'd like to dedicate this achievement to the love of my life, my husband. "Without you, I would not have been able to accomplish this." To my two little angels, Jonathon and Jordyn, "Mommy loves you, nosey-nosey-nosey!" I cannot forget family and friends. "Hey! Lets throw a party at grandma's house!" Thank you, E. Xerx and B. Andaru for making this book a better book.

NI'IHAU

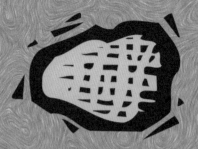

KAUA'I

NORTH SHORE

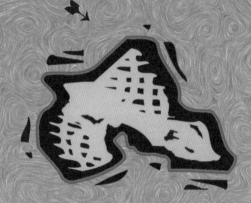

O'AHU